JASPER
& SCRUFF

THE TALENT SHOW

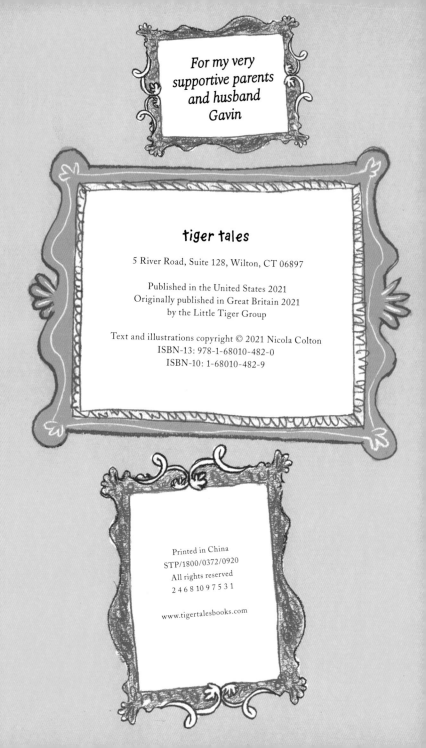

For my very supportive parents and husband Gavin

tiger tales

5 River Road, Suite 128, Wilton, CT 06897

Published in the United States 2021
Originally published in Great Britain 2021
by the Little Tiger Group

Text and illustrations copyright © 2021 Nicola Colton
ISBN-13: 978-1-68010-482-0
ISBN-10: 1-68010-482-9

Printed in China
STP/1800/0372/0920
2 4 6 8 10 9 7 5 3 1

www.tigertalesbooks.com

by Nicola Colton

JASPER
& SCRUFF

THE TALENT SHOW

tiger tales

Jasper was the type of cat who liked to look his best. So every Tuesday, he had his whiskers waxed at Ruby's salon.

Scruff was the type of puppy who liked chasing his ball through the mud. So he was always getting dirty!

One day, Jasper persuaded his best friend to come with him for a shampoo.

Scruff squirmed in his seat as Ruby lathered his fur. But Ruby knew the perfect way to calm a fidgety puppy.

"Scrub, scrubby-do.
I love a good shampoo...," she sang.

Scruff stopped wriggling and wagged his
tail in time to the rhythm.

"Wow, Ruby, you sure can carry a tune," said Jasper, admiring his newly waxed whiskers in the mirror. "Could you sing one of Alvis Pawsley's hits?"

"You're an Alvis fan?" asked Ruby. "Did you know that he's judging a talent show tomorrow?" She handed Jasper a flyer from a pile by the cash register.

REACH FUR THE STARS

Auditions at Snootington Town Hall,
Wednesday 3 p.m.
with Guest Judges:

Alvis Pawsley

Bunny Moloko

Marvello
the Magnificent

GRAND PRIZE:

Join Marvello on stage for a week
at the Velvet Theater.

Jasper remembered when he'd performed at the Velvet Theater, back in his acting days.

"Can we enter?" yapped Scruff. "I already have an idea for our act...."

"Hmm," said Jasper. "Are you going to audition, Ruby?"

"Who, me?" replied Ruby, blushing. "I'm much too shy to sing on stage."

"Come on, Jasper!" Scruff jumped up,
sending a cloud of suds into the air.
"We'd better get a move on!"

Jasper hurried home after Scruff.
As they took a shortcut through
the park...

Splash!

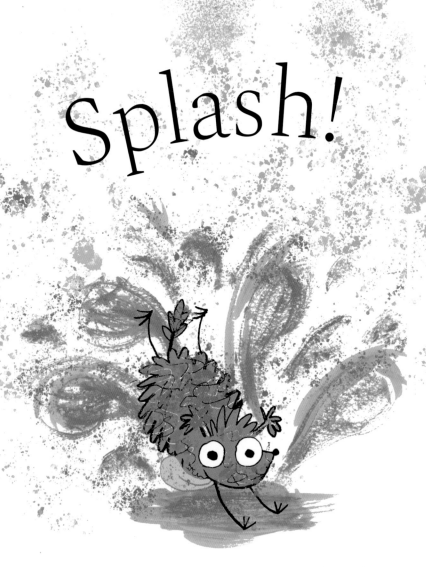

Scruff dashed through a mud puddle and dove behind a bush. Dirt flew every which way as he started to dig.

"Yuck!" said Jasper, shielding his face with his paws. "You're filthy again, Scruff!"

"Yes!" yipped Scruff. "It's still here!"

His back legs wriggled in the air as he disappeared inside the hole.

With a big heave, the puppy yanked
an old wooden box out of the ground.
He nudged off the lid with his nose
and jumped inside.

"Just watch this space and you will see...
a transformation on the count of three!"
Scruff pulled the lid back on.

"One, two, three...

Scruff sprang out of the box in
a plume of magic dust. He spun
around and tipped the top hat
that had appeared on his head.
"I am Scruff the Sensational!"

"Ugh!" said Jasper, spluttering out sparkles. "Can we stop goofing around and get home? I need to practice *my* act."

"Oh," said Scruff, his tail drooping. "I thought we could do a magic act together. I even have a spare wand."

"I'm sorry, Scruff, but I have something else in mind," said Jasper. "May the best cat win!"

The next afternoon, there was
a line all the way around the block from
Snootington Town Hall. It seemed like
the entire town had showed up
to audition!

Jasper and Scruff got in line behind

an alpaca on a unicycle.

"I'm Audrey," she said. "Ooh, are you
two doing a magic act?"

"Well, *he* is," said Jasper. "My act is
somewhat more refined."

The town clock struck three. A wave of nervous whispering swept over the line as a gazelle holding a clipboard came to get the first contestant.

"It's Salty Cyril!" said Scruff as their friend stepped through the door.

TOWN HALL

Less than a minute later Cyril was back,
his tail between his legs.

"Ahoy!" said Cyril, spotting his friends.
"I was halfway through 'Yo Ho Ho and a
Scoop o' Ice Cream' when I dropped my
drum. Marvello told me to stick to servin'
ice cream."

"That was a little mean," said Scruff as Cyril shuffled away.

"It *is* a talent show," said Jasper. "Only the best will do!"

Jasper and Scruff were almost at the front of the line when they heard a commotion behind them.

Before they knew it, Lady Catterly had pushed her way past. Reginald and Oswald followed.

"What are the Sophisticats doing here?" asked Scruff.

"No idea," groaned Jasper.

Audrey was practicing her routine one last time. As she completed a triple-twist, she spun right into Lady Catterly.

The cat's headdress wobbled.

"Watch it, you woolly galumph!" hissed Lady Catterly. "These are rare dodo feathers!"

"It was an accident," muttered Audrey. "No need to be catty."

As soon as Lady Catterly had left, Scruff turned to Audrey. "Don't worry," he said. "She's always like that."

"Shh!" said Jasper as an enchanting melody drifted out from the audition room.

"A diva with all my might..."

The voice was as smooth as silk.

"I didn't know Lady Catterly could sing!" gasped Scruff.

"Neither did I," said Jasper.

There was the sound of applause.

"Holy moly.... She's a tough act to follow!" Audrey exclaimed.
"Wish me luck."

It turned out Audrey didn't need it.
She had a huge smile on her face as
she rode out from her audition.

"I got through to the finals at the
Velvet Theater!" she cried.

"My time to shine!" said Jasper as he was called into the hall.

The three judges looked up as he flounced through the door.

REACH FUR THE STARS

"Nice outfit," said Marvello, leaning forward. "Well, show us what you've got."

"Hark! Is that a ship ahead?" began
Jasper, pulling a spyglass from his
pocket. "Three days hence, I,
Admiral Everett, will—"

"Bor-ing!" yawned Marvello.
"Next!"

"But.... I-I performed this very
speech at the Velvet Theater!"
stammered Jasper.

"Would you like to start again?" said Alvis.

"Yes, please do—" began Bunny.

"Your acting days are over!"
sneered Marvello.

Jasper flung open the door, and Scruff
bounded over. "How did it go?" he asked.

But his friend was already stomping off.

"Who's next?" called the gazelle.

Scruff gulped. Pushing his top hat
out of his eyes, he stepped into the
audition room.

A little while later, Scruff bounced into the apartment, tail wagging. "I'm in the finals!" he yipped. "Jasper?"

He found Jasper sulking inside the fort. "There you are! Marvello said my magic box was shabby, but he liked my tricks!"

"Congratulations," Jasper said through gritted teeth.

Scruff flopped down on a cushion.

"I'm sorry you didn't get in," he said.

"But why don't you be my assistant?

It'll be much more fun together!"

"Assistant? Pah!" huffed Jasper.

"I wanted to do my own act."

"I know a way to cheer you up!" said Scruff.

A few minutes later, he returned with a milkshake. "I'm sorry, but I made a bit of a mess," he admitted.

"Well, I'm sure it tastes good," said Jasper, taking a sip. He winced and spat the drink into his handkerchief. "Yuck! Is there salt in this?"

Scruff nodded. "It's salty vanilla— a new flavor I made up!"

"Let's hope you're better at making magic than milkshakes!" said Jasper. "I'm sorry for sulking. Maybe we *should* team up."

"Yay!" said Scruff, wagging his tail.

Scruff tapped a pack of cards and waved his wand. "For my first trick, I'm going to—"

"You should do it like this," interrupted Jasper, snatching the wand.

"Abracadabra, ziggedy zaggedy zoo—"

A stream of cards rushed
out and hit Jasper in the eye.
"Ow!" he yelped.

Scruff giggled.

"It's not as easy as it looks!"

"But I want to perform a trick,"
whined Jasper.

"There is something we can try,"
said Scruff. "And you'll be the star
of the show!"

"Really?" said Jasper,
straightening his bow tie.

Scruff wheeled a cat-sized box out from his room. "Climb inside!"

"No way!" said Jasper. "It's all dusty. Besides, it looks like somebody is already in there!" He prodded a pair of paws sticking out of the bottom.

"Don't worry about those for now," said Scruff, pushing them into the box.

Jasper sighed and climbed in.

"Move up to the top," said Scruff, clicking the lid shut. He pushed a button, and the fake cat paws popped back out again.

"It's really tight in here! I hope—"
Jasper fell silent as Scruff
pulled out a saw.

"What's THAT?" Jasper yelped.

"Don't worry. It's made out of cardboard," said Scruff. "But I still need you to sound scared. That's where your acting skills come in!"

"I *am* scared!" yowled Jasper as Scruff began to saw away. "I don't want to get a paper cut!"

"Ta-da!" announced Scruff.

He pushed the two halves of the box apart.

When Scruff pushed the box back together again, Jasper found that he was still very much intact.

He stepped out, his legs like jelly. "Well, that was a heart-stopping magic act! Let's hope it impresses the judges."

The pair practiced late into the night
and all the next morning, too.

*Maybe we really do have a chance of
winning*, thought Jasper as they pushed
the cat-sized box up to the theater.

Together they wheeled the heavy box down a long hallway. They stopped to catch their breath outside a door guarded by two huge gorillas.

Just as Jasper and Scruff set off again, the door swung open, and Lady Catterly stepped out.

WHAM!

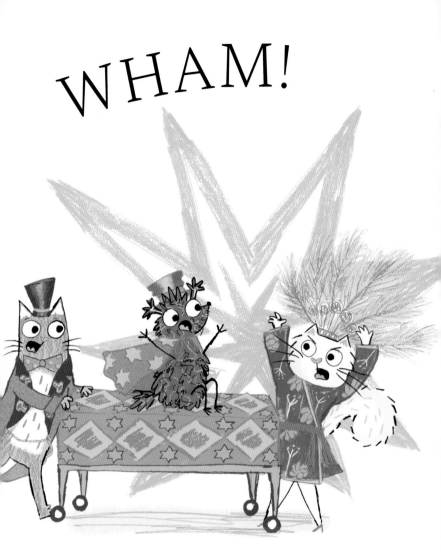

"Careful!" she hissed as the box
crashed right into her.

"Oh, I'm sorry," said Scruff.

"You will be," snickered Reginald, peering around the door.

"Ha ha, good one!" said Oswald, joining him. "Now scram!"

As Jasper and Scruff hurried into their dressing room, they could still hear the sound of the cats' laughter echoing behind them.

They found a mirror and started
to get ready.

"I think the Sophisticats are up
to something," whispered Scruff.
"We'd better keep an eye
on them."

"I'm not sure we can," said
Jasper. "Lady Catterly has
her own private dressing room."

"Will the first contestant go to the stage door!" announced the gazelle. "The show is about to begin."

"That's me!" said Audrey.

"I'm sure you'll be great!" said Scruff. "I wish we could watch."

"Scruff, you've given me an idea," said Jasper as Audrey rode off.

Jasper and Scruff
peered out
from the wings,
keeping an eye
out for anything
suspicious.

"Look! There are
the judges," said
Scruff, pointing
to a table in front
of the stage.
"But where's
Marvello?"

Bunny and Alvis jumped as the
magician appeared between them
in a puff of purple smoke.

Bang!

"Welcome to the final round of Reach Fur the Stars!" he boomed. "Tonight's lucky winner will get to perform here for a week with me, Marvello, the World's Most Famous Magician. Now for our first act!"

A spotlight fell on Audrey, who was perched on a high platform. A tightrope stretched from one side of the stage to the other. Underneath was a giant cream pie.

"If this goes wrong, things are going to get messy," whispered Jasper.

"Oh, I can't look," said Scruff. He covered his eyes as Audrey set out across the tightrope.

"That was amazing!" he said, peeking between his paws as she reached the other side.

Audrey picked up some juggling clubs and balls and edged back out onto the tightrope.

Scruff elbowed Jasper as she began to sway from side to side. "Something doesn't look quite right with the rope."

"It's coming loose!" gasped Jasper.

"Audrey!" cried Scruff. But it was too late.

"Whoa!" Audrey began to wobble. She dropped the clubs and tumbled into the giant pie.

Splat!

"Such a good start," said Bunny, dabbing her dress.

"An ambitious act. Maybe too ambitious," said Alvis, combing cream out of his hair.

"Ugh!" yowled Marvello. "My top hat is ruined! Next!"

Disco music began to play. Molly
and Milo zoomed onto the stage,
swaying in time to the beat.

"At least they have their feet on the
ground," whispered Jasper.

As the tune grew faster, Molly zipped up a ramp and shot through the air.

Milo got ready to catch her. But just as their paws met, Milo slipped.

Molly went flying toward the judges' table...

...landing right in Marvello's lap.

"Get off of me!" screeched the magician. "There are track marks all over my cape."

"Scruff! Do you see that?" said Jasper, pointing at a pool of something black and shiny in the middle of the stage.

Before Scruff had a chance to look,
the spotlight moved to
the judges.

"You just need a
little more practice,"
said Bunny.

"Um, good effort,"
said Alvis.

"I've certainly never
seen anything like
THAT before," said
Marvello. "Next!"

"We're up," said Scruff,
straightening his top hat.

"Something fishy IS going on," said
Jasper. "Keep your eyes peeled."

"For my first trick," announced Scruff,
"I'm going to saw my assistant in half."

Jasper gave a deep bow. He was about to
climb inside the box when Scruff spotted
something hurtling toward them.

"Duck!" shouted Scruff, pushing Jasper out of the way.

Smash!

A large sandbag swung into the box,
smashing it to pieces.

"Oh, no!" Jasper placed his head in his paws. "We're out of the competition."

"The show's not over yet," said Scruff. "Entertain them with some magic. I'll be back in a jiffy!" He grabbed Audrey's unicycle from the wings and sped off.

Jasper pulled out a deck of cards and
tapped them with his wand. This time,
he swished it slowly like Scruff had
shown him. The cards danced in the air.

Hmm, thought Jasper. *I don't actually
know any more tricks.*

Just then, Scruff bounded on stage
with his magic wooden box.
He held it up to show that it was empty.

"Alakazam!"

He tapped the box with his wand and a silver tray appeared, with a red velvet cake and three milkshakes.

Using their wands, Jasper and Scruff made the tray float over to the judges. Then they held paws and took a bow.

"Dazzling!" said
Bunny, taking a sip
of her milkshake.

"Spectacular!" said
Alvis, nibbling on
a cherry.

"Thah wash okay,
ashually," said
Marvello through a
mouthful of cake.

Jasper and Scruff skipped off stage,
grinning from ear to ear.

It was time for the final act.
The pair watched from the wings as
the lights dimmed and Lady Catterly
was lowered from the ceiling
on a crescent moon.

"Let's see if any accidents happen during *her* performance," muttered Jasper.

Lady Catterly shimmied to the front of the stage and picked up the microphone.

"Ain't no rival good enough,
Ain't no talent big enough,
Ain't no tricks dirty enough,
To keep me from that trophy!"

As she finished, the judges leaped to their feet to give her a standing ovation.

It was time for the winner to be announced. The contestants gathered on stage.

"It's been an, ahem … interesting final round," said Bunny. "Everyone put on a great show, but the w—"

"The winner is Lady Catterly," interrupted Marvello. "Can we all go home now? I need to change my costume."

"As I was saying...," Bunny went on, "the winner is Lady Catterly. She will be performing here tomorrow night."

"Better luck next time, darlings," trilled Lady Catterly, pushing past Jasper and Scruff to collect her trophy.

"It's no surprise that I won," she gloated. "The theater is very lucky to have me. I'm sure it will be a sell-out show...."

"The Sophisticats were behind those mishaps. I just know it," said Jasper as Lady Catterly droned on.

"Well, everyone's going to be here for a while," said Scruff. "Let's investigate."

"Good thing we discovered these air vents on our treasure hunt!" said Scruff as they climbed inside.

They crawled along until they reached Lady Catterly's dressing room. Peering through a metal grill, they spotted a box of tools.

"Oswald and Reginald must have used that wrench to loosen Audrey's tightrope," said Scruff.

"And look, a bottle of oil," said Jasper. "That's what made Milo slip and fall."

"Shh!" said Scruff. "Someone's coming!"

Lady Catterly sat down at her dressing table and removed her headdress. Jasper and Scruff couldn't believe their eyes. Sitting between her ears was Ruby!

"Oh, thank goodness," said Ruby, hopping onto the dressing table and spreading her wings. "It was very dark under there."

"Just one more week of this," said Lady Catterly. "When I—I mean, WE get a record deal, we can share the profits, and your wonderful voice will be heard all around the world."

"It was Ruby who was singing all along!" gasped Scruff. "We should tell the judges!"

"I have a better plan," replied Jasper. "Let's head over to the salon."

"Okay," said Scruff. "As long as you don't make me get another shampoo!"

The next evening, there was a huge line outside the Velvet Theater. Disguised as stagehands, Jasper and Scruff snuck in through the backstage door and hid in the wings.

MARVELLO THE MAGNIFICENT & LADY CATTERLY

The lights dimmed, and Lady Catterly
was lowered from the ceiling on the
crescent moon.

"Oooooh!"

gasped the crowd.

As the moon
drifted back up,
Marvello floated
through the air.
He hovered above
Lady Catterly,
performing a card
trick as she sang.

"Ready?" whispered Jasper.

Together Jasper and Scruff pulled
a lever. The moon started to lower,
hooking onto Lady Catterly's curls.
As they pushed the lever, the moon
rose again ... taking her wig with it!

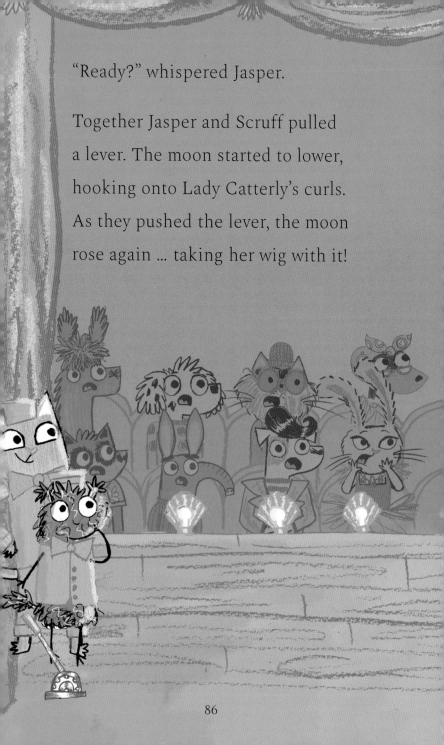

Blushing, Ruby flew up and perched
on the moon. Alone in the spotlight,
Lady Catterly continued to mouth
the words to her song, but
no sound came out.

"Boo!"

went the audience.

Lady Catterly looked around in confusion and spotted Ruby. "You've ruined my performance!" she yowled.

"*Your* performance!" cried Marvello. "You're nothing but a fluffy-tailed fraud!"

Lady Catterly picked up the microphone stand and gave Marvello a big whack. Then she stormed off the stage.

The magician swung in the air. "Get me down!" he cried as the wire holding him caught on the moon. "I am Marvello the Magnificent!"

"Show's over, I guess," said Scruff.

"Not yet," said Jasper. "The show must go on!"

Ruby performed for the rest of the evening to thunderous applause.

"Encore!" shouted the crowd as she finished her final song.

"Okay. Just one more," said Ruby. "But I'd like to invite my friends Jasper and Scruff to join me on stage."

Jasper straightened his bow tie and turned to Scruff. "It *is* much more fun when we work together."

"We make a magical double act," agreed Scruff. "Now pass me my saw!"